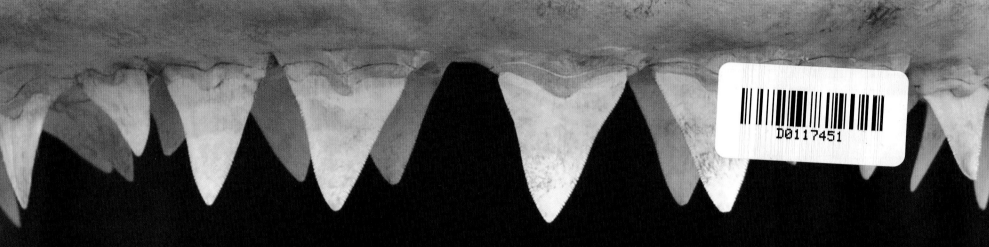

SINK YOUR TEETH INTO
SHARKS!

SCHOLASTIC

CONTENTS

SO MANY SHARKS, SO MANY TEETH 3

SHARKS!

    GREAT WHITE SHARK 6

    BULL SHARK 8

    MAKO SHARK 10

    SAND TIGER SHARK 12

    NURSE SHARK 14

    COOKIECUTTER SHARK 16

    TIGER SHARK 18

    GREENLAND SHARK 20

    SPINY DOGFISH 22

    LEMON SHARK 24

    SAWSHARK 26

    BASKING SHARK 28

    FRILLED SHARK 30

    BLUE SHARK 32

    WOBBEGONG SHARK 34

    LEOPARD SHARK 36

    GREAT HAMMERHEAD SHARK 38

    GOBLIN SHARK 40

    MEGAMOUTH SHARK 42

    WHALE SHARK 44

AN OCEAN OF PREDATORS 46

SO MANY SHARKS, SO MANY TEETH

There are more than 400 species, or types, of sharks swimming in the world's oceans. They range in size from the tiny deep-sea dwarf lanternshark, which is just over 6 inches (15 cm) long—about the size of a banana—to the huge whale shark, which is about 40 feet (12 m) long—or about the size of a school bus.

Not every shark is a big, fast hunting machine that kills and eats anything in its path. Some sharks are bottom-feeders, lying at the bottom of the sea waiting to snatch up prey. Other sharks are tiny and just take nibbles out of larger prey, such as whales. In fact, sharks' diets can be as varied as the types of sharks themselves.

MY, WHAT USEFUL TEETH YOU HAVE!

The shape of a shark's teeth is related to what it eats. Some sharks, like the great white, have big, jagged, triangular teeth. These teeth are useful for grabbing and tearing through big prey. Other sharks have thin, pointy teeth, perfect for snagging slippery prey like squid. Still other sharks have flat and ridged teeth, good for grinding clams, crabs, and other crustaceans.

TONS OF TEETH

Most sharks' jaws are filled with rows and rows of teeth. When one tooth falls out, the tooth in the next row moves into its place. Some sharks can lose about 35,000 teeth in a lifetime!

MORE THAN JUST JAWS

Though its teeth are a shark's most noticeable tools for hunting and feeding, they have plenty of other senses and skills that help them to be the great predators they are.

SUPER SENSES

- SMELL: Sharks have an excellent sense of smell. It is so good that sharks are sometimes called "swimming noses"! Their nostrils are usually located on the underside of their snout and are used only for smelling, not breathing. Some sharks can smell a single drop of blood in a million drops of water—that's like one tiny drop of perfume in a bathtub!

- HEARING: Sharks have inner ears, which means they don't stick out like a human's do. Sound travels more than four times faster in water than it does in the air, so sharks often rely on hearing to figure out if prey is nearby.

- TOUCH: Sharks have pores that run the length of their bodies. These pores are known as the lateral line. They are filled with cells with small hairs that can sense water pressure and nearby vibrations.

- SIGHT: Sharks can see well in low light. Like cats, they have reflectors in their eyes known as *tapetum lucidum*, which act like mirrors to amplify light.

OTHER HUNTING TOOLS

- CAMOUFLAGE: Many sharks have white bellies and dark-colored backs. This coloring helps them blend in to the environment. To prey looking down, the shark's dark back blends in with the dark water below. To prey looking up, the shark's white belly helps it blend in with the light water above.

- WHISKERS/BARBELS: Some sharks have whiskers, called barbels, filled with special sensors. The sharks swim close to the ocean bottom, dragging their barbels through the sand to help them detect prey.

- STAYING STILL: To breathe, many sharks must constantly move to allow water to filter through their gills. But some sharks, like nurse sharks, are able to pump water over their gills—so they can stay still at the bottom of the ocean and surprise a tasty meal!

ELECTROSENSE!

Sharks have special sensory organs known as the *ampullae of Lorenzini*. Through special jelly-filled pores in their heads and along their bodies, sharks can sense weak electrical pulses from nearby creatures. This allows them to detect hidden prey, even creatures buried in the sand.

GREAT WHITE

FAST FACTS

← 6 ft. *(1.82 m)* →

SIZE: 13–22.5 ft. *(3.9–6.8 m)*

LOCATION:
Temperate nearshore waters worldwide

WEIGHT: 1,500–5,000 lbs. *(680–2,268 kg)*

JAWS!

Great white sharks are the biggest predatory fish in the sea. These sharks are made for hunting: Their torpedo shape and strong tail let them move through the water at speeds of 25 mph (40 kph), and they have sharp senses that help them locate prey. These excellent hunters also pack a powerful bite. One team of scientists found that a 20-foot (6-m) great white shark could bite with 4,000 lbs. (1,814 kg) of force.

Shark Bite File #1

A great white's jaw contains up to 300 large, sharp, triangular teeth with jagged edges perfect for biting into large prey such as seals, sea lions, sea turtles, fish, and other marine mammals.

BULL SHARK

FAST FACTS

6 ft. (1.82 m)

SIZE: 7-11 ft. (2-3.4 m)

LOCATION:
Shallow, warm
water worldwide

WEIGHT: 200-500 lbs. (90-230 kg)

WORLD'S DEADLIEST

Did you think the most dangerous shark in the world is the great white? That scary title actually goes to the bull shark. So named because of their short, rounded noses and hot personalities, bull sharks are aggressive and patrol shallow waters along populated coastlines. They are responsible for the majority of shark attacks on humans.

Shark Bite File #2

Bull sharks' triangular, jagged teeth are great for ripping into bony fish and other sharks, but are also capable of snapping into big prey such as dolphins. These aggressive sharks will eat just about anything: crustaceans, rays, sea birds—even license plates and other junk have been found in their stomachs.

MAKO SHARK

FAST FACTS

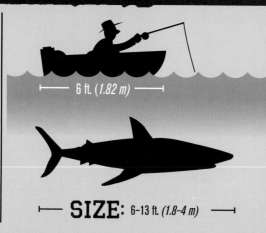

6 ft. (1.82 m)

SIZE: 6-13 ft. (1.8-4 m)

LOCATION:

Tropical and temperate waters throughout the world, and in the Pacific Ocean from Oregon to Chile

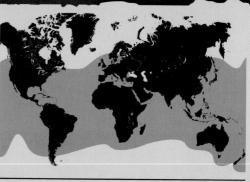

WEIGHT: 135-880 lbs. (60-400 kg)

SUPERFAST PREDATORS

Mako sharks are known to be the fastest sharks in the ocean, sometimes reaching top speeds of 60 mph (97 kph) when hunting. These superfast sharks have even been seen jumping out of the ocean. Scientists are not sure why, but some think it's part of how they hunt for food.

BEWARE!

Makos may look small compared to other sharks, but they are highly aggressive and known to attack swimmers who get in their way.

Shark Bite File #3

Mako sharks' long and pointy teeth stick out of their mouths like smooth knives. These sharp, strong teeth allow makos to easily snare quick, smooth fish.

SAND TIGER SHARK

FAST FACTS

6 ft. (1.82 m)

SIZE: 4–10 ft. (1.2–3 m)

LOCATION:
Warm waters worldwide, except for the eastern Pacific Ocean

WEIGHT: 200–350 lbs. (91–159 kg)

TAME TIGERS

Sand tiger sharks look like ferocious man-eaters: Rows of spiny teeth stick out from their open mouths, and their beady eyes eerily scan everything they see. But believe it or not, these scary-looking sharks are not aggressive and attack humans only if they're provoked. They hang out in the shallows and on the sandy sea floor and hunt prey. That's why they're named *sand* tigers.

AQUARIUM ATTRACTION

Sand tigers are some of the most popular sharks in aquariums because they do well in captivity. In the wild, their life span is usually 15 years, but in aquariums they can live longer. A shark in a New York aquarium lived to be 43.

Shark Bite File #4

Sand tiger sharks have a mouthful of thin, sharp, spiny teeth. These teeth are great for snatching small bony fish, crustaceans, and squid—to swallow whole!

NURSE SHARK

FAST FACTS

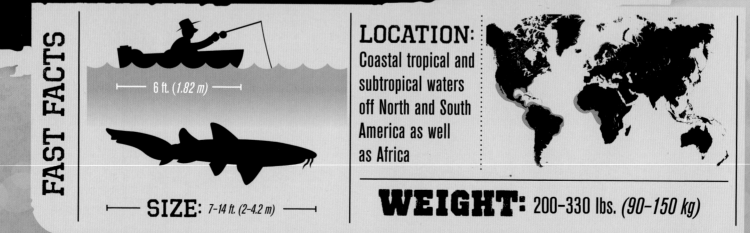

6 ft. (1.82 m)

SIZE: 7-14 ft. (2-4.2 m)

LOCATION: Coastal tropical and subtropical waters off North and South America as well as Africa

WEIGHT: 200-330 lbs. (90-150 kg)

NIGHT SHIFT

Large, slow nurse sharks spend their time at the bottom of the ocean, resting during the day on the sea floor or in caves or craggy rocks. They are sometimes found in large groups of up to 40 sharks, all piled on top of each other. At night, nurse sharks become very active and aggressively hunt prey.

WALK THIS WAY

Nurse sharks can swim like other sharks, but they also "walk" along the sea floor, supporting their bodies with their pectoral—or side—fins.

Shark Bite File #5

Nurse sharks have bumpy, fan-shaped teeth perfect for crushing and grinding shells and other tough foods. Their mouths are on the underside of their bodies so they can quickly suck up bottom-dwelling prey.

COOKIE CUTTER SHARK

FAST FACTS

6 ft. (1.82 m)

SIZE:
1.5–2 ft. (0.5–0.6 m)

LOCATION:
Warm ocean waters worldwide, usually near islands

WEIGHT: About 7 lbs. (3 kg)

GLOW-IN-THE-DARK SHARK!

Cookiecutter sharks get their name from the round, cookie-shaped bites they leave in their large prey, such as whales and seals. The ventral side, or belly, of cookiecutter sharks are lined with photophores, which are organs that produce a greenish light. Scientists think these glow-in-the-dark organs help the cookiecutters blend in with the light from the surface of the water and go unnoticed by their prey and other predators.

HUNGRY FOR A SUB?

Cookiecutter sharks sometimes munch on underwater equipment, such as cables, fishing nets, and even submarines!

Shark Bite File #6

Cookiecutters' jaws, filled with interconnected triangular teeth, can unhinge to form a circle. The sharks attach themselves to their prey with their suction-like lips, sink in their teeth, and spin around in a circle—leaving that perfect cookie-shaped bite.

17

TIGER SHARK

FAST FACTS

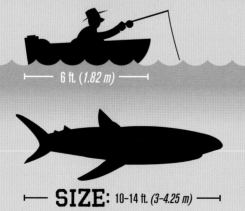

6 ft. (1.82 m)

SIZE: 10-14 ft. (3-4.25 m)

LOCATION:
Tropical and subtropical waters throughout the world

WEIGHT: 850-1,400 lbs. (380-640 kg)

UNDERWATER TIGERS

Tiger sharks get their name from the dark stripes that appear along their backs. These stripes fade as the sharks age. With a keen sense of smell and great vision, tiger sharks are excellent hunters and eat just about everything they can find, including underwater garbage!

Shark Bite File

Tiger sharks have sawlike teeth that are shaped like can openers. In one quick bite, they can easily crack the hard bones and shells of underwater prey like sea turtles.

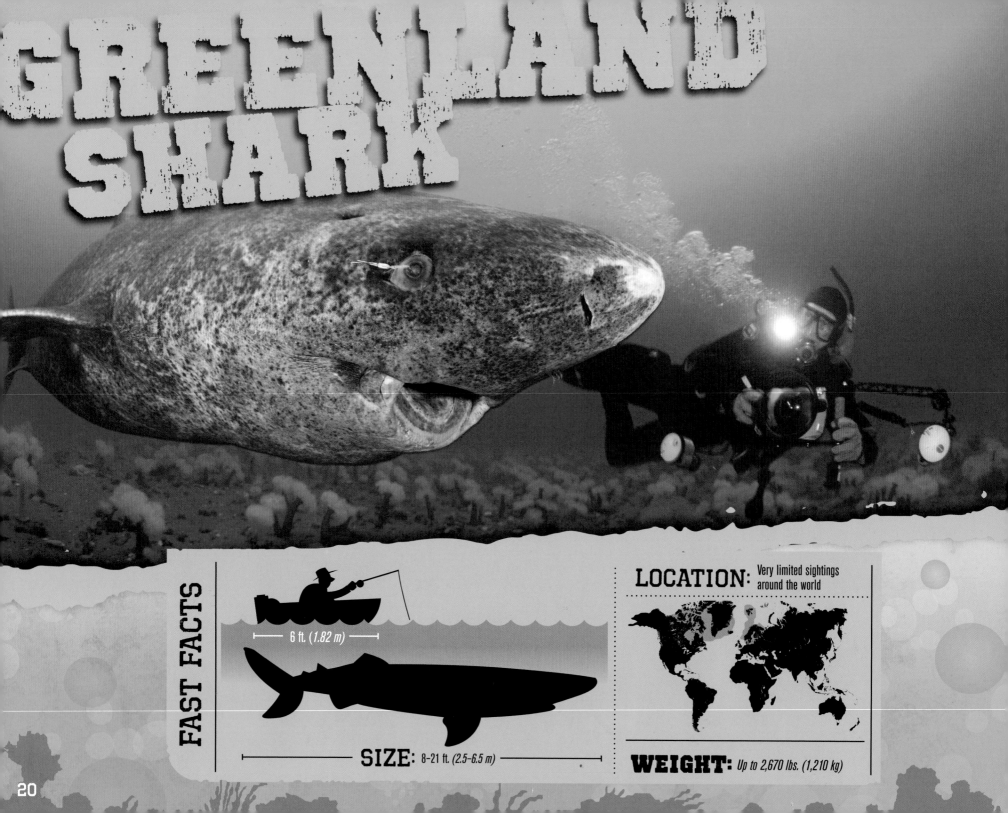

GREENLAND SHARK

FAST FACTS

6 ft. (1.82 m)

SIZE: 8-21 ft. (2.5-6.5 m)

LOCATION: Very limited sightings around the world

WEIGHT: Up to 2,670 lbs. (1,210 kg)

SLOW MOTIONS

The Greenland shark is the only arctic species of shark and lives in very cold waters. Also known as the sleeper shark, it is a slow mover. In fact, it's the slowest shark in the sea. Some scientists think that these sharks swim so slowly that they can sneak up on snoozing seals, who like to sleep in the water to avoid polar bears. Now, that's one sluggish shark!

Shark Bite File #8

Greenland sharks have pointy, thin, smooth teeth in their upper jaws and broad, square teeth in their lower jaws. Scientists think these sharks sink their sharp upper teeth into their prey (fish, other sharks, and eels), and then chew in a rolling motion with their bottom teeth.

SPINY DOGFISH

FAST FACTS

6 ft. (1.82 m)

SIZE:
3-4 ft (0.9-1.2 m)

LOCATION:
Cooler waters worldwide

WEIGHT: Up to 20 lbs. (9.1 kg)

SPECIAL SPIKES

Spiny dogfish have thin, long bodies and large eyes. They use the sharp spines by their dorsal fins for defense: Spiny dogfish arch their backs and prick anything that bothers them. These sharks used to be present in great numbers, but after years of overfishing, they are vulnerable to extinction globally.

WHY THE NAME DOGFISH?

Fishermen coined the name dogfish for these sharks because they thought they chased smaller fish in packs, like wild dogs.

Shark Bite File #9

These tiny sharks have big appetites, gobbling up herring, mackerel, and other fish. Small, pointy teeth face the outer corners of their mouths, and their upper and lower teeth form a straight, razorlike line on each of their jaws.

LEMON SHARK

FAST FACTS

6 ft. (1.82 m)

SIZE: 8-10 ft. (2.4-3 m)

LOCATION: Subtropical shallow waters in the Atlantic and Pacific Oceans

WEIGHT: Up to 200 lbs. (90 kg)

MELLOW YELLOW

Lemon sharks are so named because of their yellowish-bronze coloring. These large sharks live in shallow waters around coral reefs and mangroves, large trees that grow in coastal waters. Lemon sharks have poor eyesight and rely on their other senses—especially their electroreceptors, which sense other animals' electric fields—to hunt.

Shark Bite File #10

Narrow and triangular with smooth points and jagged bases, lemon shark teeth are perfect for crunching into bony fish and crustaceans.

SAWSHARK

FAST FACTS

6 ft. (1.82 m)

SIZE:
About 5.6 ft. (1.7 m)

LOCATION:
Mostly in waters near South Africa, Australia, and Japan

WEIGHT: UNKNOWN

A TOOTHY NOSE

These wild-looking sharks are named after their snouts lined with sharp teeth, which resemble saws. Sawsharks are often confused with sawfish, and for good reason: They both sport long, sawlike noses. There are big differences, though. Sawfish are a type of ray and have gill slits on their undersides. Sawsharks have gill slits on their sides, like sharks do. Either way, watch out for that nose!

SPECIAL SENSORS

Sawsharks have long organs that look like whiskers, called barbels, that they drag along the sand. Sensors in the barbels allow them to locate prey.

Shark Bite File #11

Sawsharks use their toothed snouts to swipe at their prey, such as shrimp, worms, and shellfish, wounding or stunning the animals so the sawsharks can turn around and gobble them up.

BASKING SHARK

FAST FACTS

6 ft. (1.82 m)

SIZE: 22–30 ft. (6.7–9 m)

LOCATION: Coastal arctic and temperate waters worldwide

WEIGHT: About 11,000 lbs. (5,180 kg)

GENTLE GIANTS

Basking sharks can be huge, reaching lengths of close to 40 ft. (12 m)—that's almost as big as a school bus! These massive sharks have hundreds of tiny teeth, but they don't use them for biting. Basking sharks are primarily filter-feeders. They have huge gill slits that go almost completely around their heads, filtering up to 2,000 tons (1,812 mTs) of water in an hour.

THE MORE THE MERRIER

Unlike most sharks, which prefer to be alone, basking sharks often form groups, or schools. These schools can be made up of a few sharks or up to 100!

Shark Bite File #12

Basking sharks open their massive mouths—which can reach up to nearly 4 ft. (1.2 m)—and swim to eat, straining small fish, eggs, and plankton through little screens called gill rakers.

FRILLED SHARK

FAST FACTS

6 ft. (1.82 m)

SIZE:
6-6 ft. (2 m)

LOCATION:
Cold deep waters at
the bottom of the
ocean

WEIGHT: UNKNOWN

Named for its frilly-looking gill slits that allow it to breathe in great ocean depths, the frilled shark is rarely seen alive. Long and eel-like, they usually surface only after they have died. These deep-dwelling sharks are called "living fossils" because they have many primitive features that haven't changed in millions of years.

Shark Bite File

Frilled sharks have large mouths full of 25 rows of multi-pronged, needle-sharp teeth. These teeth make it hard for octopus, squid, and other cephalopods to break loose once the frilled shark sinks its teeth in.

BLUE SHARK

FAST FACTS

6 ft. (1.82 m)

SIZE: 6-12.6 ft. (1.8-3.8 m)

LOCATION: Temperate ocean waters worldwide

WEIGHT: 60-120 lbs. (27-55 kg)

DEEP BLUES

Blue sharks are known for their thin bodies and extra-long pectoral fins. They also have large eyes and a long nose. They get their name from the deep blue color on their backs and bright blue sides; their bellies are white. These colors give a blue shark its camouflage in the open ocean.

WORLD TRAVELERS

Blue sharks swim long distances—more than a thousand miles (1,609 km) a year. One blue shark tagged by scientists traveled more than 3,700 mi. (5,955 km), from New York to Brazil.

Shark Bite File #14

Blue sharks have sharp, pointed teeth with jagged edges, which help them catch slippery prey, such as squid. They also eat fish—and pretty much anything else that looks tasty.

WOBBEGONG SHARK

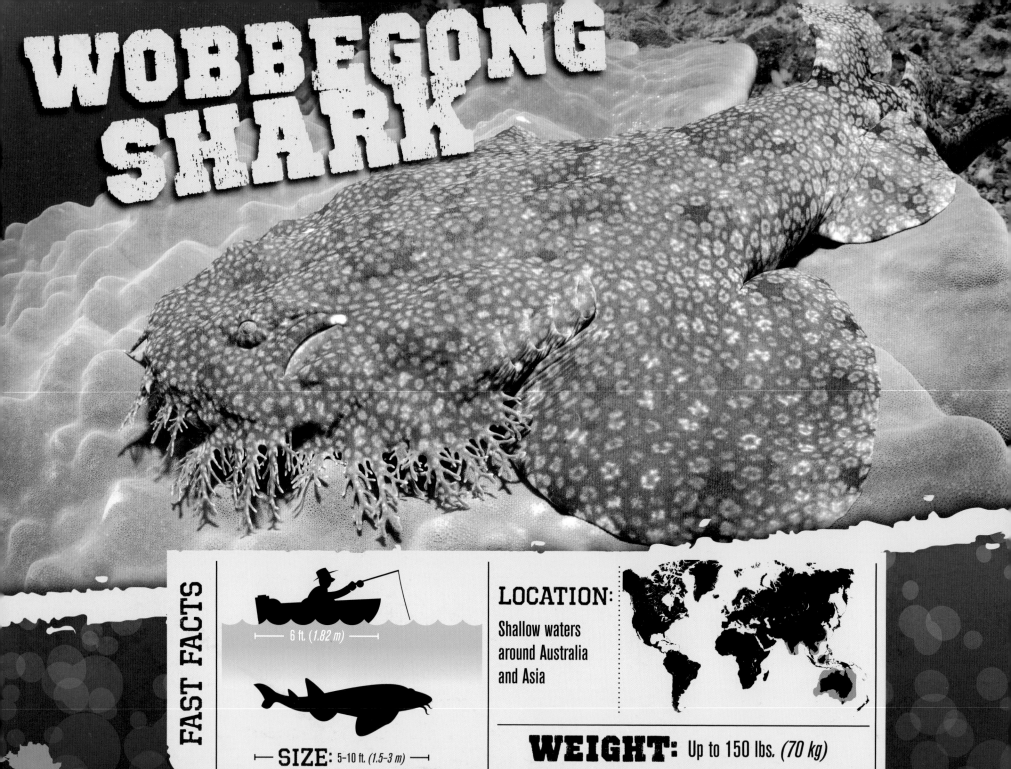

FAST FACTS

6 ft. (1.82 m)

SIZE: 5-10 ft. (1.5-3 m)

LOCATION:
Shallow waters around Australia and Asia

WEIGHT: Up to 150 lbs. (70 kg)

HIDDEN HUNTERS

Wobbegong sharks are a type of carpet shark, with flat bodies and a mottled pattern on their skin. These large sharks use their strange looks to their advantage. Their skin markings and frills help them blend into the sea floor and reefs, where they lie very still until prey swims by. Then they bite!

Shark Bite File #15

Wobbegong sharks have super-sharp teeth, often described as fangs. These night feeders hunt bottom-dwelling animals such as crabs and lobsters, as well as octopus and larger fish like sea bass.

LEOPARD SHARK

FAST FACTS

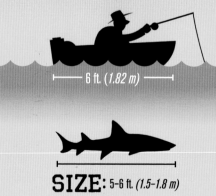

6 ft. (1.82 m)

SIZE: 5-6 ft. (1.5-1.8 m)

LOCATION:
Cool and warm
waters along the
U.S. Pacific coast

WEIGHT: Up to 41 lbs. (18.6 kg)

SHARK PARTY!

Leopard sharks get their name from the spotted pattern on their grayish-bronze backs that resembles the pattern on a leopard's coat. They are social sharks that form large schools with other leopard sharks of the same age and gender. These big schools sometimes even hang out with other sharks, such as smoothhounds or spiny dogfish.

Shark Bite File #16

Leopard sharks' smooth-edged, overlapping teeth are good for crushing and grinding. Good nibbles are crab, shrimp, clams, ocean worms, and anchovies.

GREAT HAMMERHEAD SHARK

FAST FACTS

6 ft. (1.82 m)

SIZE: 11.5 ft.–20 ft. (3.5–6 m)

LOCATION:
Tropical waters worldwide

WEIGHT: 500–990 lbs. (227–450 kg)

HANDY HAMMERHEADS

Great hammerheads are the largest type of hammerhead sharks, identified by their straight, wide heads. Their hammer-shaped noggins are called cephalofoils. Scientists think cephalofoils have many different uses. They may help the sharks swim better, sense prey more easily with spread-out electrical sensors in their nose, or help them to pin down their favorite prey, stingrays. Yum!

STINGING SUPPER

One of the great hammerhead's favorite foods is the stingray, which it eats whole—tail and all. Stingray tail barbs are often found stuck in great hammerheads' mouths.

Shark Bite File #17

Great hammerheads aren't picky eaters and will gobble up many marine animals, from lobsters to fish and stingrays to octopus and even other sharks—including other hammerheads!

GOBLIN SHARK

FAST FACTS

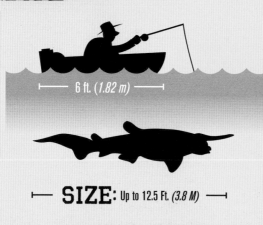

6 ft. (1.82 m)

SIZE: Up to 12.5 Ft. (3.8 M)

LOCATION:
Off seamounts and continental shelves worldwide

WEIGHT: Up to 460 lbs. (208 kg)

GHOSTLY GOBBLER

You can't miss a goblin shark. With its long, flat nose, tiny eyes, and soft, pinkish body, goblin sharks are definitely one of a kind. They are also very rare deep-sea dwellers. Only 50 have been seen since they were first discovered in the late 1800s.

Shark Bite File #18

When swimming, goblin sharks have a triangular profile. But when they attack, their jaws are shot forward by special ligaments, allowing their pointed teeth to snare fish, shrimp, and squid.

MEGAMOUTH SHARK

FAST FACTS

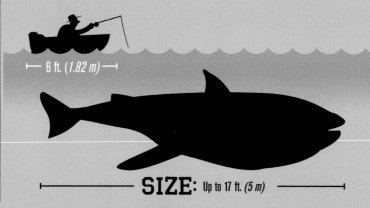

6 ft. (1.82 m)

SIZE: Up to 17 ft. (5 m)

LOCATION: Very limited sightings around the world

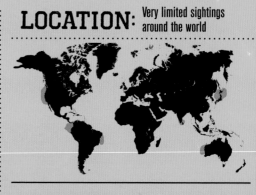

WEIGHT: Up to 2,670 lbs. (1,210 kg)

MYSTERIOUS MEGAMOUTH

Very little is known about this rare shark. In fact, only 55 of them have ever been seen or caught since they were first discovered in 1976. Here's some of what scientists do know: Megamouth sharks live deep down in the water and may sometimes travel upward at night to feed. They have huge mouths (hence the name) and rubbery lips. They're not the best swimmers—they're kind of slow and awkward.

Shark Bite File #19

The megamouth is a filter-feeder. It opens and extends its huge jaws to let in water filled with small and microscopic creatures, like krill and plankton. The water then filters out through its gills while the shark's screenlike gill rakers hold in the food.

43

WHALE SHARK

FAST FACTS

6 ft. *(1.82 m)*

SIZE: 20-30 ft. *(6-9 m)* and bigger!

LOCATION: All warm tropical waters except the Mediterranean

WEIGHT: Average 21 tons *(19 tonnes)*

SUPERSIZE SHARK

Whale sharks are not related to whales, but they are just about as big. The largest species of shark, and the largest fish in the sea, these giants average about 20–30 ft. (6–9 m) long. The largest ever measured was over 40 ft. (12 m), and scientists think they grow even bigger, maybe even up to 65 ft. (20 m). That's the length of two buses parked end to end!

Shark Bite File #20

Whale sharks' jaws can be up to 5 feet (1.5 m) wide and hold about 300 rows of teeth. But those teeth are tiny and do not appear to play a part in the shark's diet. These supersize filter-feeders eat microscopic plankton or small schooling fish.

AN OCEAN OF PREDATORS

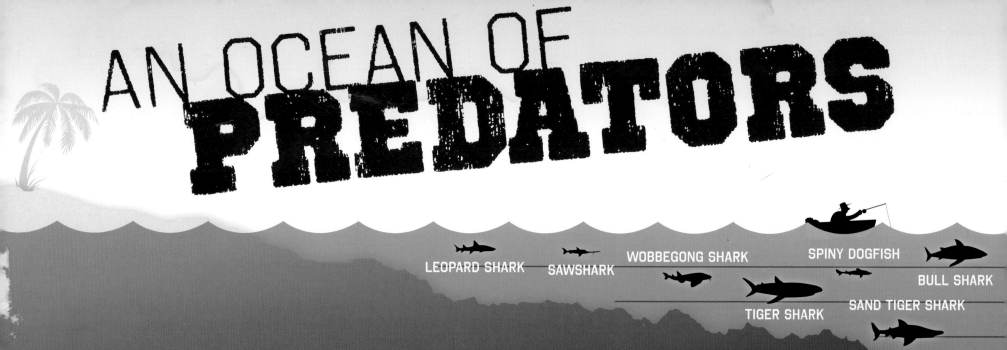

LEOPARD SHARK   SAWSHARK   WOBBEGONG SHARK   SPINY DOGFISH

TIGER SHARK   SAND TIGER SHARK   BULL SHARK

There are about 400 species of sharks that swim the oceans, and more are being discovered all the time. This diagram shows the depths at which some of the sharks in this book have been observed in the world's oceans, from the mako, which cruises in the open sea, to the tiger shark, which can swim close to shore.

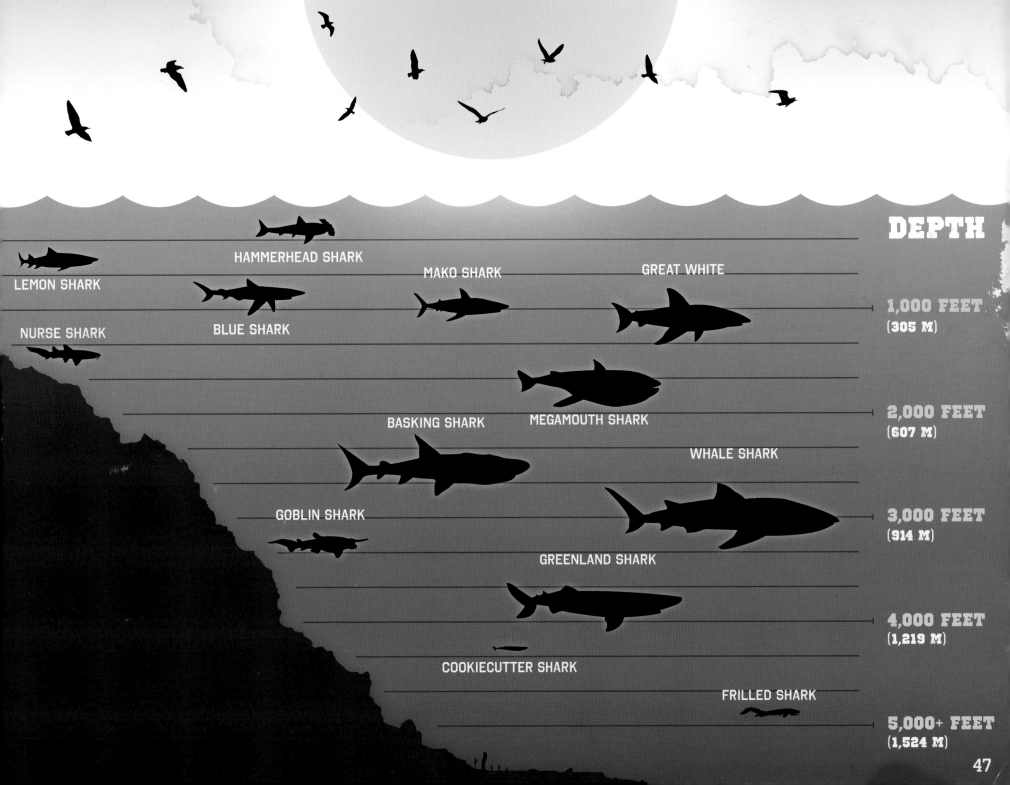

DEPTH

LEMON SHARK

HAMMERHEAD SHARK

MAKO SHARK

GREAT WHITE

NURSE SHARK

BLUE SHARK

1,000 FEET
(305 M)

BASKING SHARK

MEGAMOUTH SHARK

2,000 FEET
(607 M)

WHALE SHARK

GOBLIN SHARK

3,000 FEET
(914 M)

GREENLAND SHARK

4,000 FEET
(1,219 M)

COOKIECUTTER SHARK

FRILLED SHARK

5,000+ FEET
(1,524 M)

Published by Tangerine Press, an imprint of Scholastic, Inc.
557 Broadway, New York, NY 10012
Scholastic Canada Ltd. Markham, Ontario

Scholastic Canada Ltd., Markham, Ontario
Scholastic New Zealand Ltd., Greenmount, Auckland
Scholastic Australia Pty. Ltd, Gosford NSW
Grolier International, Inc., Makati City, Philippines

Produced by becker&mayer!, Bellevue, Washington.
www.beckermayer.com
14136

If you have questions or comments about this product, please visit www.beckermayer.com/customerservice and click on Customer Service Request Form.

Author: LJ Tracosas
Editor: Leah Jenness
Designer: Sam Dawson
Photo researcher: Kara Stokes
Product developer: Peter Schumacher
Production coordinator: Jen Marx
Managing Editor: Michael del Rosario

Sink Your Teeth Into Sharks! Image Credits

Cover: Great white shark © SeaPics.com. Title page: Shark teeth © Pinosub/Shutterstock. Page 3: Great white shark © Jim Agronick/Shutterstock. Page 4: Mako shark teeth © Kelvin Aitkin/Visual&Written SL/Alamy; blue shark teeth © Mark Conlin/Alamy; goblin shark teeth © SeaPics; tiger shark teeth © SeaPics; great white shark teeth © SeaPics.com. Page 5: Caribbean reef shark © Rich Carey/Shutterstock. Page 6: Great white shark © James D Watt/Stephen Frink Collection/Alamy. Page 7: Great white shark teeth, same as page 4; great white shark close up © SeaPics.com. Page 8: Bull shark © Michael Patrick O'Neill/Alamy. Page 9: Bull shark teeth © NORBERT WU/MINDEN PICTURES/National Geographic Creative; bull shark open mouth © SeaPics.com. Page 10: Mako shark © Mark Conlin/Alamy. Page 11: Mako shark teeth, same as page 4; mako shark open mouth © Andy Murch/Visuals Unlimited/Corbis. Page 12: Sand tiger shark © SeaPics.com. Page 13: Sand tiger teeth © SeaPics.com. Page 14: Nurse shark © Stephen Frink/Stephen Frink Collection/Alamy. Page 15: Nurse shark teeth © Scubazoo/RGM Ventures LLC dba SuperStock/Alamy; nurse shark © SeaPics.com. Page 16: Cookiecutter shark © Courtesy George Burgess. Page 17: Cookiecutter shark © Courtesy Karsten Hartel/Marine Fisheries Review/NOAA via Wikimedia Commons; cookiecutter shark bite © SeaPics.com. Page 18: Tiger shark © JIM ABERNETHY/National Geographic Creative. Page 19: Tiger shark teeth, same as page 4; tiger shark grin © Franco Banfi/Getty Images. Page 20: Greenland shark © SeaPics.com. Page 21: Greenland shark mouth © WaterFram/Alamy. Page 22: Spiny dogfish © Andy Murch/Visuals Unlimited, Inc./Getty Images. Page 23: Spiny dogfish close up © SeaPics.com. Page 24: Lemon shark © SeaPics.com. Page 25: Lemon shark teeth © SeaPics; lemon shark mouth © SeaPics.com. Page 26: Sawshark © Mary Snyderman/Stephen Frink Collection/Alamy. Page 27: Sawshark teeth, same as page 26; sawshark toothy nose © Mary Snyderman/Stephen Frink Collection/Alamy. Page 28: Basking shark © SeaPics.com. Page 29: Basking shark open mouth © SeaPics.com. Page 30: Frilled shark © SeaPics.com. Page 31: Frilled shark body © Getty Images/Staff/Getty Images. Page 32: Blue shark © SeaPics.com. Page 33: Blue shark open mouth © JIM ABERNETHY/National Geographic Creative; blue shark teeth, same as page 4. Page 34: Wobbegong shark © WaterFrame/Alamy. Page 35: Wobbegong shark close up © Jeff Rotman/Oxford Scientific/Getty Images; wobbegong shark open mouth © SeaPics.com. Page 36: Leopard shark © SeaPics.com. Page 37: Leopard shark mouth © Felix Choo/Alamy; leopard shark teeth © SeaPics.com. Page 38: Great hammerhead shark © SeaPics.com. Page 39: Great hammerhead shark open mouth © SeaPics.com; great hammerhead shark teeth © SeaPics.com. Page 40: Goblin shark © SeaPics.com. Page 41: Goblin shark mouth © SeaPics.com; goblin shark teeth, same as page 4. Page 42: Megamouth shark © SeaPics.com. Page 43: Megamouth closeup © SeaPics.com; megamouth teeth © SeaPics.com. Page 44: Whale shark feeding © SeaPics.com. Page 45: Whale shark open mouth © MAURICIO HANDLER/National Geographic Creative; whale shark mouth close up © SeaPics.com. Page 48: Shark © Willyam Bradberry/Shutterstock.

Design elements used throughout:

Abstract circles © javi merino/Shutterstock; tropical plant silhouettes © OKSANA/Shutterstock; seagull silhouette © SCOTTCHAN/Shutterstock; underwater tropical reef © EpicStockMedia/Shutterstock.

Manufactured in Shenzhen, China
10 9 8 7 6 5 4 3 2
ISBN: 978-0-545-60332-4
Complies with CPSIA
Printed in Shenzhen, China